em  ji

PHANTOM
OF THE OPERA

Brimming with creative inspiration, how-to projects, and useful
information to enrich your everyday life, Quarto Knows is a favorite
destination for those pursuing their interests and passions. Visit our
site and dig deeper with our books into your area of interest:
Quarto Creates, Quarto Cooks, Quarto Homes, Quarto Lives,
Quarto Drives, Quarto Explores, Quarto Gifts, or Quarto Kids.

First published in 2017 by Race Point Publishing, an imprint of The Quarto Group,
142 West 36th Street, 4th Floor, New York, NY 10018, USA
T (212) 779-4972 **F** (212) 779-6058 **www.QuartoKnows.com**

Race Point titles are also available at discount for retail, wholesale, promotional, and bulk purchase.
For details, contact the Special Sales Manager by email at specialsales@quarto.com or by mail
at The Quarto Group, Attn: Special Sales Manager, 401 Second Avenue North, Suite 310,
Minneapolis, MN 55401, USA.

10 9 8 7 6 5 4 3 2 1

ISBN: 978-1-63106-428-9

Editorial Director: Jeannine Dillon
Managing Editor: Erin Canning
Project Editor: Jason Chappell
Design: Ashley Prine

Printed in China

MIX
Paper from
responsible sources
FSC® C104723
www.fsc.org

em  ji
PHANTOM
OF THE OPERA

GASTON LEROUX

Sent from my iPhone

Race Point
PUBLISHING

CAST

ERIK
The Phantom

CHRISTINE DAAÉ
The Hot Singer
Everyone Wants

RAOUL, VICOMTE
DE CHAGNY
The Lover Boy and Hero

RICHARD FIRMIN
The Hot-Headed
House Manager

ARMAND MONCHARMIN
The Oh-So-Nonchalant
House Manager

THE PERSIAN
The Mystery Man

PHILIPPE, COMTE
DE CHAGNY
The Heroic Brother

MADAME VALERIUS
The Not-So-Great Guardian

MADAME GIRY
The Keeper of the Boxes

MERCIER
The Super-Scared
Stage Manager

GABRIEL
The Incredulous
Chorus Master

DEBIENNE
The Old House
Manager

POLIGNY
The Older House
Manager

LA SORELLI
The Lead Ballerina

JAMMES
A Regular Ballerina

JAMMES' MOTHER
Essentially
Unessential

MEG GIRY
Yet Another Ballerina

CARLOTTA
The Old Singer
Everyone
Is So Over

**INSPECTOR
MIFROID**
The So-So Cop

GASTON LEROUX
The Author

OPERA HOUSE
Haunted AF

Prologue

uys, the Phantom, HE'S TOTALLY REAL! I'm serious. I didn't believe it at first either, but then I met the guy who was the inspector on the (SPOILER ALERT!) kidnapping of Christine Daaé, the disappearance of the Vicomte de Chagny, AND the death of his elder brother, Count Philippe. Not to mention the "suicide" of that poor scenery changer. Anyway, the inspector told me to talk to this guy called "the Persian" (racist much!?) who showed me these texts that totally matched these other texts from Christine and they all prove—*PROVE!!!*—that the phantom was a real dude. You heard me, DUDE! Not a ghost, but a flesh-and-blood guy living on the lake under the Opera, being absolutely French-fried bananas. (YES, there is a lake under the Opera. Duh!)

Don't believe me yet? Well, remember that corpse they dug up in the basement? It was NOT, as the papers said, a corpse from that weird Commune-massacre-whatever thing, but it was IN FACT the body of the "ghost" and I can prove it! But not until later b/c I don't want to spoil EVERYTHING. Just one more adieu before the story: Shout out to all my Opera peeps who helped me piece together this dreadful and veracious story!! OK, I now present to you in all its terror-ific detail, *THE PHANTOM OF THE OPERA*, or, *THE LOVE-SICK NUT JOB IN THE BASEMENT!*

—

- Fri, Jan 10, 6:12 PM -

 🦴 !!!!!!!!!!!! 😵 👻 😵 👻 ☠️ ⚰️ 👻

 Don't be an idiot! 😈 . . . Did you see it!?!?!

 With my own 👀 !!! And I think he stole my powder puff the other day. 😞 😞

Ugh, no one has actually seen the ! Now leave me alone. I have to write my speech for 🎩 and 😠's going-away party tonight! 🤚 🤐

I SAW IT!!! And what about the scene changer, Joseph Buquet!? He 👀 the 👻 and said it had a 💀 for a head and no nose!!! 🙀💅 And he's too boring to make that 💩 up.

AND 🧔, he saw him too and he was wearing fancy clothes!! 🎩

Why was 🧔 wearing fancy clothes?

NO!!!! THE GHOST WAS!!!!!!  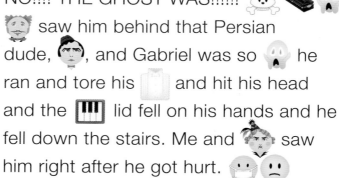 saw him behind that Persian dude, and Gabriel was so he ran and tore his and hit his head and the lid fell on his hands and he fell down the stairs. Me and saw him right after he got hurt.

Are you still talking?

– Fri, Jan 10, 6:15 PM –

The is here!!!!!!

 It's true! My mom says he

 •••

 Never mind. I shouldn't say it.

What!?!? What does say!?

I shouldn't tell you . . . but . . . well, is in charge of box 5  and she says that management told her to reserve it . . . for the !!!!!!! He goes there every night and she can't SEE him 👀 but she can HEAR 👂 him !!! And she even gives him a program! 🌙 📰 👻

🙁

– Fri, Jan 10, 6:17 PM –

BOUQUET IS DEAD!!!!!
⚰️⚰️⚰️ 😢 💀

Why are you so upset about some dead flowers? And who the heck gave you flowers anyway!?

No no no, JOSEPH BUQUET!! Stupid autocorrect. He was found hanging under the stage next to a farm set.

It had to be the !!!!

TOTALLY!!!!

TOTALLY!!!!

is magnificent tonight!

 OMG!!! She passed out!!!!

You look like you're the one about to keel over!

 Let's go make sure she's OK.

Um, what?

LET'S GO!!!!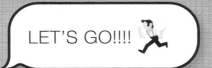

Oooooooookkkkkk . . .

- Fri, Jan 10, 6:24 PM -

 You sure seem to know your way to her  . . .

Just keep up!

I think I'll just let you go check on her. I'm going to go see ! 😄

Whatever!

- Fri, Jan 10, 6:37 PM -

 Did you hear 🌼 sing tonight!?!? Like an 😇 !!!

Right? And just 6 months ago she sounded more like a dying 🐮! 😛

LOL! Can't believe she passed out. My pretty brother went chasing after her. ♥♥♥

Jeez! And did you hear about the dead guy?!?!?!

 What!?!? Tonight's friggen !

- Fri, Jan 10, 6:38 PM -

 Are you OK!?!?!?!?!?

Who dis?

Oh, um, remember that kid who fished your scarf out of the ocean?

Hahaha, ooookkkk . . .

Wow. Burn. Anyway, can we talk??

Later, when I feel better.

- Fri, Jan 10, 6:40 PM -

YOU HAVE TO 🖤🖤🖤 ME!!!!

Ugh, how can you say that? Did you not hear me 💃 tonight??? FOR YOU!!! ☹️

Sigh, you're right. Your singing was enough to make 😇 😨. Thank you. 🙏

- Fri, Jan 10, 6:45 PM -

Aaaaah!!!!! Do you see the 👻 !?!?!?!?

NO! And now everyone is in an uproar. and 🎩 left before I could finish my speech, and I DON'T SEE ANY 👻 !!!

You didn't see that guy with the 💀 FOR A HEAD!?!?! You know, with the BLACK HOLES FOR EYES!!?!?!?! 👻

No. I did not. Speech ruined. 😈

Those shrieking  are right. Buquet's death might not be such a natural thing. 😜

Say what!? Joseph Buquet is dead?????

Oh yes. Found hanging between some sets in the basement. 🪢 Tragic.

😱😟

From: Debienne 😐, Poligny

To: Armand Moncharmin 😶, Richard Firmin

Subject: The Basics

Dear Messieurs,

We do hope you'll enjoy running our little 🏛! Few things. You'll want to get new master keys made! Very important! Trust us.

Next, you'll want to read the memo of terms from the government. The 🏛 is a state operation, so, you know, bureaucracy! Basically it just says you need to "exhibit the splendor that befits the foremost lyric theater in France 🇫🇷." Failure to do so will end in you being fired. 💧 No pressure! 😐

You'll notice that there's a peculiar handwritten clause in the memo about, well, the 👻. He's the only one allowed in 📦 5, and he gets 20,000 💵 each month. 💰 💸

Sounds strange, we know, but trust us, you want to make sure 👻 = 🙂!

Sincerely,
Debienne 😐 and Poligny

From: Armand Moncharmin , Richard Firmin

To: Debienne , Poligny

Subject: RE: The Basics

You're joking, right?

From: Debienne , Poligny

To: Armand Moncharmin , Richard Firmin

Subject: RE: RE: The Basics

Nope. Don't believe us?
You will!

- Fri, Jan 10, 9:12 PM -

Those guys are hilarious!!! 😛😄 Glad someone still has the good ol' French sense of humor these days. 🇫🇷

Ugh. Fools! When this "ghost" shows up, I'll just have him arrested. 💂

For sure! They're giving up so much 💰, it's 🤑.

And we're renting that dang !

 Oh definitely!

 be damned!

 Was a pretty funny gag though!

From: P. of the Opera

To: Armand Moncharmin , Richard Firmin

Subject: Sorry to bother you, but . . .

Hey,

I know you guys are super busy right now, planning the fate of the 🏛️, signing contracts, getting new acts, whatever. I feel I *have* to tell you that 👸 can't sing for 💩. 🐱 only has one ASSet 😊 😄. 😵 dances like a 🐄. But for some reason you've given them all great roles, while 🦁 goes unnoticed. Are you blind 😐 👀, deaf 😐 👂, or just stupid? But whatever—you are free to do what you want.

I'm really writing to remind you about reserving my 📦 for me and giving me my 💰 💰 💰. I thought maybe 🎩 and 👴 forgot to mention those things to you, but they assure me they did. So, you know, DO IT!

Your devoted servant,
P. of the O.

- Sat, Jan 25, 11:32 AM -

 Those guys really can keep a joke going!

Ugh. Right? If they think we're going to reserve that for them 4ever just because they used to be directors, they're 🌰🌰!!

If 👴 and 🎩 want 💰, why don't they just ASK!? I'm getting really sick of this 👻🐂💩!!!

Eh, they probably just want the tonight. Let's just give it to them.

I guess. . . . But man, did you see what they said about , 🐱, and 🌸? YIKES!

I know! But they 🖤🖤🌼 for some reason. Maybe, you know, they LIKED working with her?? Wink wink, nudge nudge! 😉

 You know just as well as I do that she's got the reputation of an 👼.

Maybe that's just a rumor. Maybe she's really a 😈!!! People think I know everything about music, and I don't know 💩!!

Don't worry, no one thinks that about you. 😛

From: P. of the Opera

To: Armand Moncharmin , Richard Firmin 😠

Subject: Thanks so much!

Hey guys,

Last night was pretty good. Chorus needs work. 👸 was meh. She's fine, just not special. You know what I mean? Anyway! The 🎩 was great, and I'll let you know soon how you can get me my 💰. 🎩 and 👴 paid me for the first 10 days of the year, so that means you only owe me, let's see, 233,424 💵 for the rest of the year. 👍 😃

P. of the O. OUT!

- Sun, Jan 26, 10:08 AM -

Thanks for inviting me and to use the  last night! Much as we'd to Faust AGAIN, we already told you, that belongs to the ! READ THE MEMO!!!

- Sun, Jan 26, 10:10 AM -

Those guys are pissing me off!!

Seriously! And did you hear about this from last night!? The house manager had to call the and kick out whoever was in 5. I got a whole long report about it. Dang drunks!!

WHAT!?! Let me have a talk with that guy . . .

- Mon, Jan 27, 10:12 AM -

WTF happened the other night!?!?

Oh, well, um, did you see the report? ?

I want YOU to tell me what happened.

OK, so, I guess they probably had a few too many 🍻.

The people in 🎭 5 claimed a voice told them their 🎭 was already occupied when they tried to go in. So they asked the attendant 🧑 to check if anyone was there. There wasn't. Obvs. Anyway, they kept making a racket, so I had to kick them out. The attendant thinks it was the 👻, of course. LOL!

Have you ever seen this !?!?!

What, me? No . . .

 Too bad for you! I'm firing anyone who hasn't seen him! 🔥🔥🔥 Since he is EVERYWHERE, and EVERYONE has seen him, if YOU haven't seen him, you must not be doing your job!

- Mon, Jan 27, 10:20 AM -

 Madame Giry? This is Richard Firmin.

I know who you are. We've texted about my daughter, . REMEMBER!?

No idea what you're talking about. Anyway, tell me what happened last night. Why did you and call the 👮?

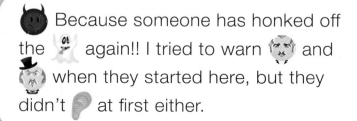 Because someone has honked off the 👻 again!! I tried to warn 👴 and 🎩 when they started here, but they didn't 👂 at first either.

Have you ever spoken to this so-called ?

Of course! What a voice!! First time I him, he said he was the phantom of the opera, told me not to be , and asked for a footstool. I went into the but no one was there or anywhere around it either. So I gave him a footstool! Now we're pals. He leaves me and sometimes ! Good guy. He even listens when I tell everyone to turn off their phones. I swear, he's the only one in the audience who does!

OMG! Please just shut up!!

- Mon, Jan 27, 10:34 AM -

 That old  is !

 her?

- Tue, Jan 28, 2:48 PM -

 Hi! Maybe I could stop by sometime to say hi? ✋

Who dis? JK! Scarf guy, right? Anyway, sorry, busy. I'm going to Perros tomorrow. It's the anniversary of my dad's death, RIP, and I'm going to visit his 🪦 ⛪ 🙁. You know, he really liked you . . . you totally shouldn't come! 😉

- Wed, Jan 29, 8:32 AM -

 Hey! I'm at the Auberge du Soleil-Couchant. 🖤 this inn! So close to the s!

I already know you're here.

 How?

Dad told me.

 Did he also tell you that I you?

LOL! That's !

Don't laugh!

I didn't want you to come here to tell me that kind of stuff.

But you DID want me to come. You knew telling me would make me come, and why do you think I'd do that unless I 🖤 you!?! 🐟

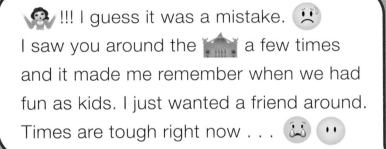

🙈 !!! I guess it was a mistake. 😥 I saw you around the 🏛️ a few times and it made me remember when we had fun as kids. I just wanted a friend around. Times are tough right now . . . 😭 😶

So you saw me before that night in your ▪, after you fainted??

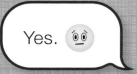

Yes.

 I knew it!!! Why did you pretend you didn't recognize me!?!?!

 Well, I'll tell you why! It's because there was another dude in your dressing room with you, and you didn't want him to think you 🖤 me!

If anyone upset me, it was you! You're the one I kicked out, remember!?!?

That's because you wanted to be alone with HIM! "Did you not hear me tonight??? FOR YOU!!!" Ring a !? What about "YOU HAVE TO ♥ ME!"

You looked at my texts!?!?!?

Gotta run!

Listen, I have to tell you something super serious. Do you remember the Angel of Music?

Sure I do! Your dad told us about it all the time.

Remember how Dad said that once he's in heaven, he'd send the to me? Well, he's in heaven, and the Angel of Music has come to me!!

Sounds right to me! No human could sing like you did the other night. Something like an had to teach you to sing that way.

Exactly! The comes to my dressing room and teaches me to sing every day!

In your DRESSING ROOM . . . !?!?!

Yup!

Has anyone else heard this ???

 You saw his texts from that night.

LOL!

 WTF are you laughing at!?!? You think it was just some random dude?

Oh, for sure it was! Don't you??

 What kind of girl do you think I am!?

I think you're awesome! But I also think someone is playing a trick on you.

 UGH! Just leave me alone!!! I never want to talk to you again!!!!

I you turned up half dead, half frozen on the steps of the 🏛️ in Perros last night because you were following 🐑 around. 🙁 Did she notice you following her?

No, but I thought she would. I was stomping along in the ❄️, making noise, hoping she'd turn to see me. She never did. I guess she was lost in thought? 👣❄️ I followed her to the 🏛️ and the ⚰️⚰️⚰️⚰️⚰️.

 Are you superstitious?

Yes! No! . . . Maybe?

 Hmmmm, were you feeling, how should I say, ??

Nope . . . I was upset that 🦁 was wandering alone, but I thought she just wanted to see her dad's 🏛️. She didn't 👂 me, and I didn't want to disturb her 🙏. Then this amazing 🎻 🎵 🎶 started that sounded just like how her dad played when we were kids. Standing there with all those 🏛️🏛️ and 💀💀💀💀 was definitely freaky!

And when the 🎻 🎵 stopped?

👱‍♀️ left, and then a 💀 rolled off a pile of bones and landed at my feet!!! 🧔 I guessed the mystery musician knocked it down, and I saw a shadow, so I chased it. 🏃 He turned around, and I swear, he had a 💀 for a face!!! I thought it was the 😈! I was so freaked that I keeled over and don't remember anything until I woke up at the inn. 👻👻👻

- Fri, Jan 31, 10:40 AM -

 Let's go take a look at this 5 for ourselves.

- Fri, Jan 31, 10:51 AM -

 Holy !! DID YOU SEE THAT!?!?!

YES!!!

 Ugh, that ! Gruesome!

??? I saw an old lady. Looked like . . .

That's weird. I saw a sitting on the ledge.

Let's go back for another .

 Someone is trying to trick us and make fools out of us!

Tomorrow we're watching the show from 5 to figure this out.

From: P. of the Opera

To: Armand Moncharmin , Richard Firmin

Subject: Is it war you want? ???

Cuz we can have a war! ●●●
If that's NOT what you want, then here are my conditions:

1. [box] 5 = mine. All the time. Starting now. ⌚

2. [singer] sings lead tonight. [dancer] Don't worry, [girl] will be indisposed. 😈

3. [girl] is awesome! 👍👍👍 You will unfire her.

4. Give my 💰💰💰 to [girl], K? Thx.

If you don't do these super-easy things, well, let's just say I WILL CURSE
THE 💩💩💩💩💩 OUT OF THIS PLACE!!!!!!!!!!!!!!!

P. of the O.

Morning, boss. So, um, did you hear about Cesar?

WTF are you talking about!?!?!? I AM IN NO MOOD!!!!

 Oh, uh, the 🏛️'s prized horse 🐎, Cesar?

The

Oh, yes, we need specially trained for the stage and parades and stuff. And Cesar was the best! 😍

OK, so what about this magical Cesar??

He was kidnapped . . . Horsenapped?

You're joking!

 I wish. I really that !

Well, who the would horsenap Cesar!?!

 The of course!

ARE YOU AN IDIOT!?!?! I would you right now if you didn't work for the government!!!

From: px9247spambot479r@anonemail.com

To: Carlotta

Subject: Tonight

If you 🎤 tonight, I'm warning you, something bad will happen. Like, really bad. REALLY REALLY BAD! Like worse than death bad!!!! 🪦🪦🪦 ☠️☠️☠️☠️☠️

From: px9247spambot479r@anonemail.com

To: Carlotta

Subject: Achoo!

Too bad you're so sick tonight 😷 with such a bad cold. 😷😷😷 YOU COULD NOT POSSIBLY SING!! 🎤🎤 You'd be 🤢 if you did!!!

From: Carlotta 🧑‍🦱

To: px9247spambot479r@anonemail.com

Subject: RE: Achoo!

Ugh, 👱‍♀️, it is SO OBVIOUS that it's you doing this! I feel freaking FANTASTIC! 🖤 And not only will I sing AWESOMELY *TONIGHT*, but all of my friends will be there. Whatever your silly little plan is to take my place singing lead, well, I wouldn't even bother. 🌚 🕷 🔋 ☠️

From: Mailer Daemon

To: Carlotta 🧑‍🦱

Subject: Delivery Failure Notification

FATAL ERROR: Delivery to the following recipient failed permanently:
px9247spambot479r@anonemail.com

- Sat, Feb 1, 7:09 PM -

 First act down, and no !

Seems like the is late!

 Classy audience tonight, too! Especially for a place with curse on it! 😄😄 Except for that bunch down there.

HA! That's my personal concierge and her brothers. I'm replacing with her.

Er, you know is going to file a complaint against you, right????

With who? The !?!?!? LOL!!!

- Sat, Feb 1, 8:14 PM -

 Walking around during intermission was a waste of time! And now I'm tired!

Well, it gave the 👻 time to leave some 🍬 in the 🎰 for us. 🙂

 Ugh, HATE! And now 🐑 is bleating like a 🐮 on stage. I can't believe the so-called 👻 wants her to sing lead.

- Sat, Feb 1, 8:18 PM -

 Am I going 🥴, or did 💃 just make a 🐸 croaking noise!? Not like a flat 🎶, but the actual sound a 🐸 makes!?!?!?!

SHE DID ‼️⁉️ WTF ‼️⁉️

 Not to be double paranoid, but is there someone here in the 🏚️ with us?

OMG!! YES!! I am too scared to even turn around!! 👻👻👻👻👻👻👻

- Sat, Feb 1, 8:21 PM -

 Wow, 👸 is singing like 💩. It's enough to bring down the 🕯️!!! 😃😈

Who is this!?!?!?!?!

Oh, I think you know!

- Sat, Feb 1, 8:24 PM-

DO YOU SEE THE MOVING

AAAAAAAAAAHHHHHHHHH!!!!!!!!!!!!!

fell on my concierge!!!!!!!!!!!!!!!!!!!! MY CONCIERGE IS DEAD!!!!!!! 💀⚰️💀⚰️

Did you get a text right before it fell? About 👰 singing badly enough to . . .

To bring down the !? YES! 👻🙁😵

- Sun, Feb 16, 2:56 PM -

Hi! Long time, no 👀. I heard 👱‍♀️ has been staying with you . . . Has she been home lately?? She hasn't been at the 🏛 for like 2 weeks. 🙁💔

Raoul! It's so good to hear from you!  is with her , of course!

Seriously!?

Yes! But you can't tell anyone.

You can trust me.

I know it! Oh, Raoul, I you so much! And so does !

Really!? What did she say about me!?

 She told me how you told her you  her. 😊 😃!

 😠😠😠

 Oh, don't be mad. You're just so YOUNG! And it's not your fault that you thought 👱‍♀️ was a free woman.

 What? Is she engaged 💍?!

Oh heavens no, but she's not allowed to marry.

 Why the not!?!

Because the   forbids it, silly! Well, not technically. He doesn't say "I forbid you"! But he did tell her if she were to get married, he'd stop teaching her. And she doesn't want to lose an !!!

 WTF!? Is she, you know , with him??

WHAT!?!? Of course not!!! That girl is as pure as , you raunchy boy! LOL! He just gives her  lessons.

Where does this live!?

In heaven! DUH!

UGH! 🙄 Well, where does he give 👱‍♀️ her lessons?

In her early in the morning. But she's pure as and don't you forget it!!!!

Riiiiiiiiiiiight. I'm sure it's an and not some sweet-talking dandy from the !!! 😠 😠 😠

I'm glad you understand. 🙂

- Sun, Feb 16, 4:43 PM -

You look like 💩! I'm taking you out for dinner.

Nah, no thanks.

Are you sure??? We can go to a place near where was spotted last night in a with some dude . . .

For realz!?

Yup!!!

Let's go already!!!!

- Sun, Feb 16, 10:24 PM -

Hey! I think I just saw you go by in a ! I'm at the park, too!!!!

- Sun, Feb 16, 10:28 PM -

Hello . . . Christine????

- Sun, Feb 16, 10:43 PM -

CHRISTINE!!!!!!! 💔💔💔💔💔

Service Error 323: DELIVERY FAILED.

From: c974NigerianPrince7ex@anonemail.com

To: Raoul

Subject: I need you!!!

Hey,

Meet me at the 🏛 for the masked ball on Wednesday at midnight. ⌚ Which I guess is technically Thursday?? W.E. Wear a white mask and meet me in the small salon near the door leading to the rotunda. DON'T TELL ANYONE!!! 🤐 And don't get recognized!!! 🙊👀 If you don't come, I will literally DIE!!! 🗡💀🗡💀🗡

Christine 🙅

- Thur, Feb 20, 12:00 AM -

 Is that you in the black mask??

Yes! Follow me and 🤐 !!

 But who's that dude shouting about being the Red Death?! ☠️ 👻 He looks so familiar . . . OMG!! I saw that 💀 in Perros!!!!!

Ugh, did you make eye contact? Cuz now he's following us. Good job! 👍 😡

 He's not getting away from me this time!!!!

In the name of our ❤️❤️❤️, don't go after him!!!

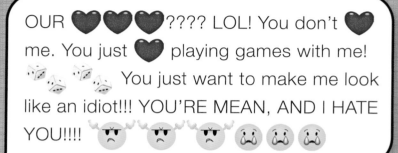 OUR 🖤🖤🖤???? LOL! You don't 🖤 me. You just 🖤 playing games with me! 🎲🎲 You just want to make me look like an idiot!!! YOU'RE MEAN, AND I HATE YOU!!!! 😠 😠 😠 😥 😥 😥

One day you'll be sorry you said that, and when you are, I'll forgive you. 🙏 That's just the kind of girl I am. 😠

Yeah, right! You drive me !!! And to think I was going to give a mere 💁 my super-prestigious family name. I'm so embarrassed, I could die!!! 😳 ⚰️ ☠️
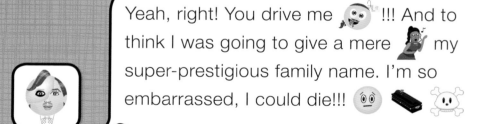

You know, I asked you to meet me so I could explain all this to you, but I can see now that you'd never believe me. It's over between us!! Good day, sir!

WHAT!?! You can't say that and then NOT tell me!! You've been missing for 2 WEEKS!!! All you tell 😊 is that it's your 👼 🎵 . Well, you know what? I think someone's tricking you and it's about time you wake up! ⏰ Now tell me WTF is going on around here!!!

Sigh, one day maybe. Now I've got to go. DO NOT FOLLOW ME!!!

On my way home!!!

Really!?!?! What about your   ??

 Let us never speak of him again. Agreed?

But he gave you lessons for all those months!

If I promise to tell you about it one day, will you for now???

- Thur, Feb 20, 3:20 PM -

Have you heard from ??

Why of course! She's home with me now. Her sent her back to us. Wearing a no less!!!

That dude is dangerous!  Tricking her cuz she's so sweet. He's no !

- Thur, Feb 20, 3:22 PM -

 You have scared silly! You have to promise you won't disappear again! 🙏

Ugh, why did you tell her all that stuff! I'm a free woman, and you don't tell me what to do! Just stop sticking your into my business! #smashthepatriarchy The only person who could ever have any say in what I do is my husband, and I'm NEVER getting married! NEVER!!

Oh, is that so!? Then why are you wearing a !?

That? Oh, that's nothing. Just a gift.

Someone gave you as "just a gift"?? HA! If you accept a as a gift, that means you accepted the proposal!! DUH!

That's my business, not yours. Now I'm sick of all these questions!

It may not be my BUSINESS, but don't act like I have no right to be concerned about you after what I saw last night.

Meaning what exactly?

I heard you going, "Oh, poor Erik!" Then when some voice started singing, you were all !!! And then you DISAPPEARED INTO A MIRROR!!!! WTF!?!?!

OMG! Were you spying on me AGAIN!?! You creep!!! If I do another guy, it's not your business!! How are you not getting that!?

He doesn't deserve your !
He's tricking you into thinking he's some kind of !

And so either he must be evil, or I must be an idiot, is that it???

 Um, I wouldn't have said it quite like that . . . 😳

Listen, you don't know it, but you're dancing with death. 🕴️⚰️💀 I know you think you have some right to me, but just leave it! I mean it!

 Only if you promise to hang out with me sometimes. Just as friends. 🤞😬

Um, ooookkkk. We can hang out tomorrow if you want.

 Really!?!?! Sweet!! OK, I promise to stop sticking my in!

Please don't mention noses again! 😃

- Fri, Feb 21, 12:16 PM -

 So, you know I'm going to ⛵ to the North Pole in like 3 weeks. 🙁

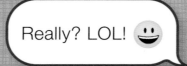
Really? LOL! 😃

 How can you be so mean!?! We might NEVER see each other again. 😭 😟 💔 I could DIE!! 🔋 ☠️

Sigh, me too. We probably won't ever see each other again after you leave. Wait!! I have an idea!! 😃👏😃👏😃👏

 Why is me dying making you so 😃?

No, silly, that's not it. OK, so we could never be married, right? 🙇🏻‍♀️💍🙇🏻‍♀️

Um, I think we could 💍, but you're the one who says we can't . . .

Shut up and listen! 🤐👂 We can't get MARRIED 🙇🏻‍♀️🙇🏻‍♀️ but we can get ENGAGED! 💍👍 A secret engagement! Then no one could possibly get hurt! Deal???

Um, you're 🥴 but YES! Christine, will you marry me!?!?! 💍⛪🙇🏻‍♀️

 Yes!!! 🎉🖤👏😄🙂👍
🖤🖤🖤🖤🖤

- Sun, Mar 1, 2:08 PM -

 Being engaged to you has been the best week of my life! 🖤💖😃 You know, I don't think I'll go to the North Pole after all.

Say what now . . . ? 👻🙂

- Mon, Mar 2, 10:17 AM -

 Have you seen ? I can't get in touch with her . . .

Oh yes, she left here around 5 yesterday. Said she'd be gone for a couple of days.

 What!? Where did she go!?!?!?!

No idea. And that's 's business, you nosy boy!

You know, I'm starting to think you're not the best guardian.

- Wed, Mar 4, 9:32 PM -

You're back!!!!! And you sang like an 😇 tonight!!!! It was incredible!!! 🖤👏👏👏 I'm glad 👰 quit after that 🐸 incident, so you can be the lead now!

I sang for you tonight. 🙇‍♀️🎵🖤 I can't hang right now, but come to my 🚪 tomorrow.

- Thur, Mar 5, 1:10 PM -

So, where have you been?

Who, me? Nowhere, never mind that! Let's meet up in a few days. 👣 This place has the coolest stuff! We'll go up into the rafters. It's like being up in the sky! 🕸 😃

- Mon, Mar 9, 5:06 PM -

How come we always go up into the top part of the 🏛? Why don't we go down, into a trapdoor 🚪? I hear weird 💩 goes on down there . . .

Nuh-uh, no way, NEVER! I forbid it!   Don't you ever go down there!!!! Everything down there is HIS.

So HE lives down there, does he!?!?

What?!?! Who said that?? Sometimes I think you're ! Let's go up to the roof. 😃

Did you see that!?!? A trapdoor just slammed shut!

So? It was, uh, one of the trap-shutters. It's what they DO! They just go around opening and shutting trapdoors 🔲. Nothing weird about that!!! You're 🌰 if you think otherwise! 😶

 But what if it was HIM‼️⁉️

No way, he's working. And he can't be working AND going around shutting trapdoors 🔲. Duh! When he works, he doesn't 🍴🙆🥂🙆😴💤 or anything, so he certainly doesn't have time to go around shutting 🔲. So stop worrying! 🫨😄

Listen, if you don't tell me WTF is going on with this 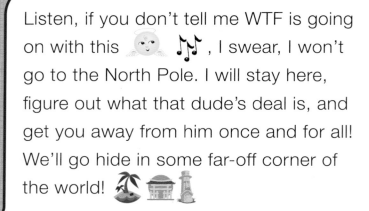 , I swear, I won't go to the North Pole. I will stay here, figure out what that dude's deal is, and get you away from him once and for all! We'll go hide in some far-off corner of the world!

- Mon, Mar 9, 5:57 PM -

There is no place more beautiful to see a sunset than from here on the roof of the !! . . . When it comes time to run off to or wherevs, I might . . . resist. If I do, promise you'll drag me, by force if you have to . . .

Ummmmm, OK . . . Do you think you're going to change your mind or something???

  that is actually the !! And if I go back to his underground lair, who knows what will happen!

Well, why the F would you go back

If I don't, awful things could happen.  And if I don't go to him, he'll come and get me!!! And then he'll 😢 and tell me he 🖤 me, and then I'll HAVE to stay!! BLECH!!! If I see that creepy 💀 face of his cry again, I WILL DIE!!!

Uhhhhhhh, wow, OK. Classic manipulator!!! Why don't we just go right now!?!?!? Like this very second!!!

I have to stay and at least let him me again tomorrow. After all, he spent all that time teaching me. We'll go tomorrow after the show. Meet me in my 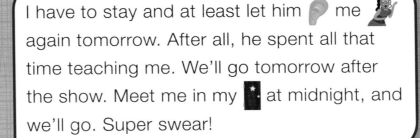 at midnight, and we'll go. Super swear!

Did you hear that?

It sounded like somebody dying or crying or something . . . 😵 😭 I'm sure it's nothing. Tell me about how you met 💀 face!

OK, I heard gorgeous singing 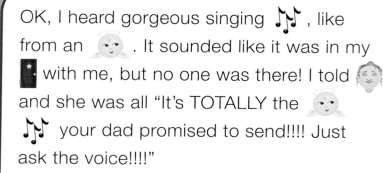, like from an 😇. It sounded like it was in my 🚪 with me, but no one was there! I told 👩 and she was all "It's TOTALLY the 😇 🎶 your dad promised to send!!!! Just ask the voice!!!!"

Way to go, 👩! 😠

So I asked, "Are you the 😇 🎶?" and the voice was like "YESSSSSS!!! OBVIOUSLY YES!!!! I came down to 🌍 to teach you to 🎤. That's absolutely it!!!"

Ok . . .

 So he started giving me lessons and after a while, my singing became like his, like an !!! I didn't even recognize my own voice. It was kinda freaky TBH! But said I was too sweet to fall for a trick by the . . .

You know I 🖤 but she's not exactly the sharpest knife in the drawer.

Right!?!?! Anyway, then you came along and I told the voice how happy I was to see you. 😃 🎉 But he was 😡 !!! He said if I 🖤 you, then he would have to go back to heaven! 👣 🌀 So I promised him that u + me = 🙅. Then I realized that my 👼 was JEALOUS and an 👼 probably wouldn't be jealous . . .

So why didn't you cut him off when you figured it out?

Because I didn't figure it all out at once, and then, the bad started! singing like a , the thing. I admit, when it fell, I was afraid for you AND him, so I knew then that I you both!

Super.

Well, I saw you in your 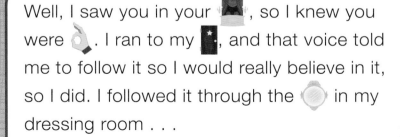, so I knew you were 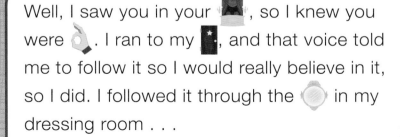. I ran to my 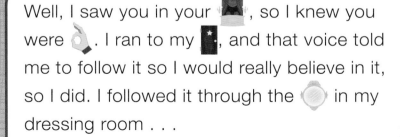, and that voice told me to follow it so I would really believe in it, so I did. I followed it through the 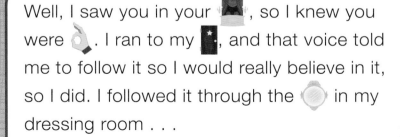 in my dressing room . . .

Are you sure you weren't dreaming??

Don't be a ! You saw me disappear into the yourself! After I went through, I was in some dark passageway and a bony hand grabbed mine. I screamed my brains out! Then I saw , wearing a mask that I could have sworn I'd seen in some heavily copyrighted opera . . .Then a bony hand covered my mouth, and I passed out.

GROoooooooooooOOOOOossssss
SSSSSSSSSSSSS!!!!

I KNOW!!! SO GROSS! When I woke up, he was dabbing my head with a cool towel. Which was sweet? Maybe? But his 🤚 smelled like 🔋. Then I saw Cesar the 🐎!!! Everyone said he'd been stolen by the 👻 and I started to wonder if the 😇🎵 WAS the 👻.

Really? Just then!?! It had not so much as crossed your mind before!?!?!?! 🙄

😈 ANYWAY!!! He puts me on the 🐎 and I feel like I've been drugged maybe? 😵💊😵 ??? The 🐎 took me past all this 🔥 and these 👿👿👿👿👿.

OMG!!! That is !!

 Then we get to this on a lake—an UNDERGROUND LAKE—and rows us to the middle of it. I'm starting to come down from the and am full-on again.

How did a fit on a ??

 Focus, pretty boy!!

The didn't get on the !! 🙄😤 We go inside some weird structure, and it's posh AF in there! He tells me not to be afraid, that I'm in no danger. It's the same voice from my lessons, so I definitely know it was not an 😇 but just some dude!!!

My turn! 😒😒😒😒😒😒

Whatevs! I reach up to take off his mask, and he says I'm not in danger so long as I DO NOT TOUCH THE MASK! OK, fine. Then he admits he's not an or anything, just a dude named Erik!

Did you just hear something? It's getting really dark, and this dude sounds MEGA CREEPY SCARY!!! I'm telling you, we should leave RIGHT NOW!!!

NO! I have to finish my story first! And if I leave before I sing tomorrow night, he'll DIE! Then again, he'd kill us just as likely as he'd kill himself . . .

OMG!!! This is ridic! He's a PERSON! We could just go and find him and talk to him! Reason with him!

 Go REASON with the guy who drugged me , put me on a , and rowed me to his subterranean mansion to force me to him!?

UGH!!! I really hate !!! Don't you!?!

 No, I don't hate him . . .

Well, if you ❤️ him so much, why don't you marry him‼️⁉️💍👰😈

 Way to be cool about all this! 😶 Listen, he TERRIFIES me!!! But I don't hate him. I feel bad for him. After he kidnapped me, he felt bad 😰 and said I could go free if I wanted to.

Oh, well, that just makes him a stand-up guy then, I guess! 🙄

Are you forgetting this is the guy who taught me to sing like an ?? I am an opera singer. That is MY LIFE! And he gave me the thing I wanted most in the whole .

OK, FINE!

So I stayed and we sang and he played music, and he didn't try to touch me, and it was definitely WEIRD, but it wasn't horrible. Then when I woke up the next morning, and reality set in, I was like, WAIT, this is 🌰!!! I have to get out of here!!!

Thank goodness!!! I was starting to wonder . . . ???

So I start freaking out on him, telling him to take off his . He was all, "You will NEVER see Erik's face!!!" and I HATE when people talk about themselves in the third person.

Ugh, it's the worst!

He says if I stay there for 5 days, then I won't be 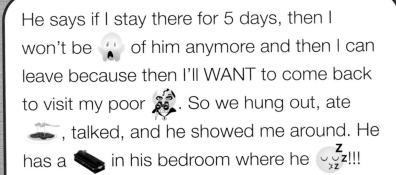 of him anymore and then I can leave because then I'll WANT to come back to visit my poor . So we hung out, ate , talked, and he showed me around. He has a in his bedroom where he !!!

His bedroom????

And he has a HUGE organ!!!

It takes up the whole wall. It's where he composes 🎵.

He is working on his masterpiece, "Don Juan #Winning!" and when he's done with it, he'll take it into his 🔋 and DIE!!! Anyway, that 🎭 was really bugging me! We kept hanging out and playing music, and at one point, I was so into the 🎵 that I sort of lost it and ripped off the mask!!! 😳

OMG!!!! What did he look like!?!?!?!?

 It was HORRIBLE! Like dried up 💩 on a bad stretch of road. Like wax dripping off a deformed dead 🐗. Oh, the HORROR!!!! 😩👻😩👻😩👻

Oh, barf!!!!! 😩😵 Ha, I bet his organ doesn't look so big anymore!

Then he said some misogynistic 🐂💩 and just freaked out. He said that since I had seen his horrible face, I could never leave, and he threatened to make a ⚰️ big enough for both of us!! 😰👻 Then he slithered off to his bedroom 🐍 and sobbed and wailed.

And you want to stay because you feel BAD for this guy???

But wait! There's more!

MORE!?!?!?! OMG. Do you give a rose to every guy you meet?

Then I heard him start to play his amazing "Don Juan #Winning," and all other  is utter compared to that. So I told him I wanted to see his face, and I promised not to because his  genius was way hotter  than his face was ugly.

Sooooo, you were able to overlook him lying about being an sent by your father, having a 💀 face, being kidnapped and drugged, and promises of imprisoning you UNTIL YOU DIE AND ARE BURIED IN A 🪦 WITH HIM, because he rocks out hard on the 🎹? Did I get that right?

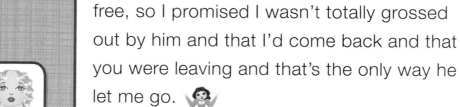

Listen, I had to be cool so he would set me free, so I promised I wasn't totally grossed out by him and that I'd come back and that you were leaving and that's the only way he let me go. 👸

But you DID go back.

I did. You should have seen him crying!!!  It was pitiful!

So you love/hate/are terrified of/feel bad for this dude???

YES! Exactly!

Jeez, my astrologer warned me about dating Geminis! 🙄

Let me ask you this, if he were hot , would you still me?

Ummmmm . . . Shut up and kiss me!!
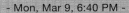

- Mon, Mar 9, 6:40 PM -

 You 2 better start running. FAST!

 Thanks! #strangerdanger

- Mon, Mar 9, 6:41 PM -

 We have to go to my , like NOW!

!?

NO! I mean RUN!!!!

OH! Don't make me act like a coward! If is here, I'll punch him right in his stupid skull face! Better yet, LET'S JUST LEAVE NOW!!!!!!!!

I CAN'T!!!! It would bring bad luck. Plus, I told him I'd only you here . . .

Oh, how very kind of him to let us hang out. How very brave you are to let us pretend to be engaged.

Oh, he knows all about the engagement! He said it was fine since you're leaving soon and to let you be as as he is in the meantime. What do you think that means??

It means that people who are in 🖤 and don't know if they are 🖤 back are MISERABLE!!!!

Are you talking about or you??

BOTH! Sigh. We're still going to leave tomorrow night, RIGHT!?

 YES!

- Tue, Mar 10, 10:02 AM -

 You see the NEWS yet?

Nope!

OH! Well, it's TERRIBLY interesting! Apparently you're engaged  to . I am VERY upset about it , but you two are SO in that I couldn't possibly stop you from going to the . Isn't that INTERESTING!?!

Don't you see she is keeping you on the hook with her stories!?!? She's making us into fools!!

I am so out of here!!!!

I know you said not to disturb you for any reason tonight, but, well, disappeared!!

So?

From ON STAGE! People are panicking!

LEAVE ME ALONE!!!!

WTF is going on around here???

It's all the !

 and are acting too!

What do you mean??

What do I mean!?!?! You don't think it's weird that they  themselves in their office and won't talk to anyone ⁉️

 I just went to tell that disappeared, and you know what he said? "GOOD FOR HER!" TELL ME THAT'S NOT WEIRD!

OK, maybe it's a little weird . . .

- Tue, Mar 10, 11:30 PM -

Christine! Where are you!?

Service Error 323: DELIVERY FAILED.

- Tue, Mar 10, 11:33 PM -

I've got a few questions for you.

CHRISTTTIIIIIIIIIINNNNNNNEEEEEEEE!!!!!!!!!!!

Riiiiight. . . Maybe I'll go talk to and for now . . .

CHRISTTIIIIINNEEEE!!!!!!

- Tue, Mar 10, 11:34 PM -

I told you we should have sent for the the first time that made us fork over 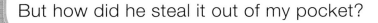! Now he's made off with our 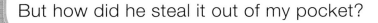 AGAIN!!!

But how did he steal it out of my pocket?

Maybe HE didn't do it!!!

WHAT!?! You've been with me this whole time! Maybe YOU were the one to

- Wed, Mar 11, 12:02 AM -

 Is in your office?

Huh? No! What are you talking about??

That disappeared. From onstage!

Oh, that. Right. Sigh. I hate this job.

- Wed, Mar 11, 12:05 AM -

 An took !!

Oh boy. OK, did you see this so-called ?

 YES! In a graveyard!

Well, that is where they hang out . . .

 I know it sounds but it's the truth!!!!

I think the truth is that ran out of here like earlier because HE took so you couldn't her. You should go chase down his !

 REALLY!?!?! I'm on it!

Where the are you going!?

After my brother and !

Sigh. Thank god you're pretty. 🙁 doesn't have her, HE does. That freak is the only one who could pull that 💩 off.

OMG!!! You know 🧛!? You're the only other person who believes in him, so I am going to immediately trust you completely! 🙏😄

Good! 👍 Now we'll go to 🧑‍🦳's 📱, get my 🔫 🔫, go through the ⚪, and find that 😈 in his lair!

 Did he show you how to work the ⚪?

 No, but unemployment has its benefits and I'm familiar with that 😈's work. The 🏛 obeys him, because he built its foundation, just like he did for the Shah's palace back when I was head 👮 in Persia.

  Whoa!

Now take this and hold it up in front of you no matter what!

But it's heeaavvvyyy!

OMG. Seriously? Then just put it in your pocket and point your hand like a gun.

OK, I figured out the mirror. Now follow me. We're going to go through some secret passages. That crafty 😈 made it so he can see everyone but no one can see him. 👀 🙊

- Wed, Mar 11, 12:33 AM -

How much farther do we have to go till we get to the lake!?!?!? CHRISSSTTINNNNNNEEEEEE!!!

Oh my God, stop whining! And we can't go by the lake. HE guards it. HE almost drowned me when I tried to cross it. 🛶 👎 That freak only spared me because he recognized me.

So how DO we get in

You remember Joseph Buquet?

The guy who was found dead? 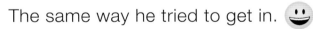 Yesssssss . . .

The same way he tried to get in. 😃

I found it! I found the way in! I just have to push this brick, a  will open, and we'll drop down into HIS lair! 😃👍

👍

Thanks for catching me . . . 😳
What's this thing on the floor . . . ?

That would be, well, the 𝄃 Buquet hanged himself by . . . 🙁

What!? And why are all the walls here made of mirrors!?!?!

I guess some guys like to watch. Actually, I think we might be in the torture chamber . . .

WHAT!?!?! And why are there 🌴 🌴🌴 in a torture chamber!?!?

Yeah, there's just one 🌴 reflected a bunch of times. And that's not a real 🌴. It's made of iron and it's here so when we go 🤖 there's something to hang the 🪢 on . . .

- Wed, Mar 11, 1:19 AM -

You've got 2 options: or 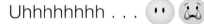 for everyone! The 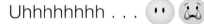 is prettttty while the option would be super ! I just want to be normal sauce, and if you marry me, then I can do that! And I'll do everything you say and make you super !

Uhhhhhhhh . . .

You don't me! Ugh, don't . It makes my ! You have until 11 tomorrow night— which I guess is technically tonight?? W.E.— to decide to me. Wait, I just heard the doorbell . . . WTF!? BRB!

Where are you!?!? Are you OK!?!?

Thank god your messages are working again!!! I can't believe I get service here . . . ! I'm fine, though I may be in a torture chamber . . .

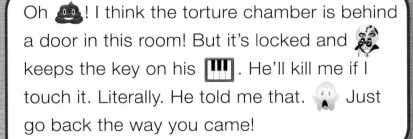

Oh 💩! I think the torture chamber is behind a door in this room! But it's locked and 🧛 keeps the key on his 🎹. He'll kill me if I touch it. Literally. He told me that. 👻 Just go back the way you came!

NO WAY! We either leave here together or die here together. 🖤🖤🖤🖤🖤

Allllright, but you know it's probably going to be the second one, right? 😟

- Wed, Mar 11, 1:23 AM -

You've got to get this door open! Try to coax HIM into giving you the key. Smile at him , be cool. Remember, he 🖤🖤 you!

Sigh. How could I ever forget? I'll try finding the key . . .

- Wed, Mar 11, 1:38 AM -

 Visitor dealt with! So rude! You know how late it is? Oh well, he won't be bothering us again.

I don't even want to know . . .

He's at the bottom of the lake! Where he'll mind his own business forever! OH! I should go play my requiem for him! 🎹🪦

Great! Yes, let's do that . . .

- Wed, Mar 11, 1:49 AM -

 Um, dearest, did you take my keys while I was playing the 🎹?

Oh, that! Yeah, I was just curious about what that torture chamber you mentioned is like. You know women, we're just so naturally inquisitive! 🙂😄😃

Well, still. Not cool. Wait, did you just 👂 something?

What? Down here? Don't be 🤪. It's just you and me. 💜

 No, I definitely 👂 something. And it's coming from the torture chamber! 😈 I bet it's someone you want to 😍! Someone with a really nice 👃! When will people born with a 👃 learn to appreciate such a beautiful gift⁉️⁉️

Honestly, I didn't a thing!

 Well, snookums, why don't you just go look through that window. I'll turn on this light, and then you can see if anyone is in there, since you're SO CURIOUS! 😈

- Wed, Mar 11, 2:01 AM -

 Man, it is REALLY hot in here with the lights on! 🔥🔥🔥

I think that may be the torture starting . . .

- Wed, Mar 11, 2:03 AM -

So, do you like the view??

There's a tropical forest in there! 🌴 🌴🌴 Neat! OK, saw it. You can turn off the lights now. 🙂

😀! Yeah, right. If you come around my torture chamber, you get the heat! 🔥🔥🔥

Let's not talk about s .

isn't answering my texts!!!! CHRISTINNNNNNEEEEEEE!!!!!

OK, you have to keep your 💩 together! Remember, we're just in a small room, and we're going to find a way out. I just have to search every square inch of these 🔥 hot mirrors with my fingers to find the secret counterweight. 😥

What about through those 🌴🌴🌴?? Maybe that's a way out?

Oh, thank goodness I found you! I've been wandering these  for days, looking for . Do you have any water? I AM SO THIRSTY!!!

 I'm thirsty too, buddy.

- Wed, Mar 11, 2:18 PM -

 Wake up! We're in a now!

 I see an oasis! Water!!

 It's just a trick.

It's not! I'm a sailor! I've 👀 the 🌑 and that was a forest, and this is a desert, and that's an oasis!!! I can 👂 the water lapping on the shore. The cool, cool water!!!

Please don't tell anyone I just licked that mirror. 🙏

I can't take it anymore. I'm done. I'm using this . Goodbye to you. Goodbye to . Goodbye to this inferno!!! 🔥🔥🔥🔥

Wait!!! I just found the way out!!

Just now? Well, that was good timing!

Seriously. I just press this nail between these floorboards and voilà!

 OMG! That cool air is AMAZING!!! Dang, there's a lot of barrels down there!

This must be 's cellar! He keeps some 👌 wine. We're saved!

 Wait, they're not filled with wine. Or water. It's gunpowder . . . 🙁

Holy ! If doesn't say yes to the dress, he's going to blow up the !!

- Wed, Mar 11, 10:55 PM -

Are you still there!?!?!?

YES! We're here!!!!

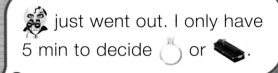 just went out. I only have 5 min to decide ⭕ or ⬛.

And not just yours. He's going to blow up the whole ! 🌑 ☠️ ⚰️ ⚰️ ⚰️ ⚰️

💩!!!! I'm supposed to turn some dumb 🦂 statue on the mantel in here if my answer is 👍 and a 🦗 statue if my answer is 👎. Obvs I have to turn the 🦂. 😥

What if it's a trick!?!? Don't turn anything!

- Wed, Mar 11, 10:59 PM -

So, what's it going to be? 🦗 of death or 🦂 of wedlock? 💀 or 🧛‍♀️? You have like 5 seconds to decide . . . ⌚ ● I'm reaching for the 🦗 . . .

FINE! Look, I'm turning the 🦂

- Wed, Mar 11, 11:06 PM -

You can tell 🧛 to turn off the water now. It's getting pretty wet in here . . .

- Wed, Mar 11, 11:08 PM -

CHRISTTTIINNNNNNEEEEEE!?!?!?!?!

- Wed, Mar 11, 11:14 PM -

Turn off the water! I saved your life once! You owe me!

Ok, ok, fine. You're lucky I owe my a wedding gift, or I'd drown you like !

One Week Later

Hey, so sorry about almost drowning you last week . . . oopsie!

Like you drowned !?

 Not my fault! He fell out of the 🛶 or something dumb. He was dead when I found him. ⚰️☠️

Well, as I was occupied in your torture chamber, I'll accept that explanation for his perfectly natural death. ⚰️☠️

And I didn't drop the either. That thing was just old.

Didn't you build this ?

 Only thing I did was use my ventriloquism skills to make that sing like a. Ok, not the ONLY thing.

W.E. Is alive!? What about !?!

Fine, don't even ask me how I am. Rude! They're both FINE! Off being and 🙂 and in 🖤. OK!?

Really??

REALLY! 🐩 is an 👼. She pitied me. Cried for me. ☹️ Don't judge me, Persian!!! Even after everything I did and even though I am pretty much a horrifying living corpse. She was sad for me and let me 💋 her forehead and she didn't even 🙈. So I gave her the as a wedding present and set her and that stupid 👃-haver free.

Wow. I almost don't regret not letting you get executed back in Persia.

Thanks? Anyway, she'll be back to bury me when I'm actually a corpse one day, which is going to be pretty soon.

Well, thanks for not murdering everyone.

 NP.

Epilogue

Three weeks later, Erik was dead.

Good story, right!? I checked it all out using notes from the Persian, and it's all TRUE. Just like I said it would be. I found all the passageways and the lake and everything, though I couldn't get inside Erik's lair. Moncharmin and Firmin eventually convinced themselves that each had pranked the other about the whole ghost-murder-extortion thing. LOL! The police and the newspapers all think the disappearance of Raoul and Christine is some great mystery. That maybe Raoul killed Philippe in some love-triangle feud, but really they just eloped and live in Sweden or something now.

And what of Erik? Do we pity him or hate him? He was born with no nose, looking like a corpse. His parents were sickened when they looked at him, so they kicked him out of the house when he was just a kid. He traveled as a sideshow in a circus for years, learning all sorts of tricks and traps. When the Persian met him, he was building a puzzle palace for the Shah of Persia, and once he was done, the Shah wanted to kill him because he knew too much. Same thing happened in Constantinople, except the Persian wasn't there to help him escape that time. That's how he became so twisted. No love, no affection, no nose, just cruelty and threats of the noose. Since God made him so ugly, I hope He also has mercy on him now. RIP, P. of the O.